Rio
Here we Come!

Penn Mullin

Cover Design and Interior Illustrations: Damon Rarey

International Standard Book Number: 1-57128-011-1

10 09 08 07 06 05 04 03 02
 0   9   8   7   6   5   4   3

You'll enjoy all the High Noon Books. Write for
a free full list of titles.

Contents

Lots of stories appeared in the newspapers after the four seventh graders in Miss Lake's class came home from their special trip to Europe. They had been given the trip by a mysterious "Mrs. X," who arranged a mystery for them in each place they visited. Marco Santos, a pilot, read about the kids and decided he wanted to show them *his* country – Brazil – and other South American countries – during their summer vacation. And he would fly them everywhere himself – in his own plane!

CHAPTER 1

Welcome to Rio!

"Wow! Rio is totally *beaches*! I can't wait to get down there!" Juan pointed down from the plane window.

"That beach is called *Copacabana* (copa-ca-BAN-a)," said Marco, their pilot. "One of my favorites in Rio. And look how white the beaches are! Did you know there are 50 miles of them in this city?"

"And we have only three days here!" Lisa groaned. "Can't we stay longer?"

"South America is so large. And we have so much of it to see," said Miss Lake, their teacher. "But I'm like you, Lisa. I want to stay longer in every place Marco takes us."

"Well, you will be back," laughed Marco. "I'm glad you like my country. First you went across America in your bus. Then Europe. When I read about this, I said to myself, 'They should see South America, too! And I have the airplane!' So, here you are! And now you are in my home city – Rio!"

"We're lucky that you read about us!" Amy said. "This is such a neat trip!"

"Marco, what's that mountain straight ahead?" asked Justin. "It is *humongous!*"

"That's *Pâo de Açúcar* (pow-day-ah-SUE-car)! Sugar Loaf Mountain. We'll go up on top of it while you're here," Marcos said.

"We're going to the top of that?" Lisa asked. "It's all rock. I don't see a road."

"There's a cable car that goes up on a wire," Marco explained. "You will love it."

"A cable car on a *wire*? I don't know about this," said Lisa.

"You'll probably never leave the beach, Lisa," laughed Justin.

"And you'll never leave the restaurants!" Lisa said.

"Can we see the big soccer stadium yet? The one where Pelé played?" asked Juan.

"*Maracana* (mara-CA-nah)? It is over there to the east," Marco pointed. "We are too low to see it now. But we will go there while you are in Rio. We are very proud of Maracana!"

"I've got to send postcards of it to some guys back home," said Juan.

"It's hard to believe Rio is part of Brazil, too," said Amy. "This is so different from the jungles we saw up north."

"Brazil is a *big* country," Miss Lake said. "Even a little larger than the United States!"

"O.K., everybody. We just got cleared to land! Seat belts tight?" Marco asked.

CHAPTER 2

City of the *Cariocas*

Marco's small twin-engine plane taxied over to the airport gate.

"That was a beautiful landing!" Miss Lake told Marco. "We touched down so softly."

"Thank you! It must be because Rio is home!" Marco laughed.

"Rio de Janeiro," Juan read on the airport tower. "What does the name mean?"

" 'River of January.' There is a funny story about how Rio was first given this name. When

Portuguese sailors discovered this bay in 1502 they thought it was the mouth of a big river. So they named it after the month of the discovery – January!" Marco explained.

"So Rio started out belonging to Portugal?" Amy asked.

"Yes, it was a Portuguese colony until 1889." Marco shut off the plane's engines. "It made Portugal very rich: The country around Rio was perfect for growing sugarcane and coffee trees. And then gold was discovered nearby in 1690. Today it is a republic with a president and individual states like your country."

"O.K., kids. Grab your backpacks," said

Miss Lake. "And clean up any wrappers or cans."

"Lisa, are you sure you can lift your backpack?" Justin asked. "It gets heavier each place we stop!"

"Well, yours is so full of food," Lisa said.

Everybody climbed down from the plane.

"Oh, it feels so good to *stretch*!"Amy said.

"And the air is wonderful," said Miss Lake. "Not too hot, just right."

"Rio has a wonderful climate. And remember – this is our winter – June!" Marco laughed. "Justin, Juan, let's unload the duffel bags."

Marco and the boys opened the baggage

holder under the plane and pulled out the duffel bags. Soon they were all walking into the airport together.

"My sister Eliana (el-i-AN-a) will meet us out front," Marco said. "She is so excited you are coming."

"It's great we can all stay with her," Amy said. "Does she have room?"

"Oh, yes. Her apartment is very large. And it is only two blocks from *Ipanema* (ee-pa-NEE-ma) Beach!" Marco said.

"Ipanema! That is so famous! All my postcards are going to be from there," Lisa said. "And we'll be only two blocks from it!"

Suddenly they saw a pretty dark-haired

woman running towards them.

"Marco!" she cried as she ran up to hug her brother. *"Bon dia* (bon-JIA) (Good day! Hi!), everyone! I am so glad you are here. I can't wait for you to meet my children, Carlos and Éva (ΛY va). They are waiting at home so we would have room for you in the van. Come, I am parked close by."

They all followed Eliana out to her van.

"Lisa, you're falling behind!" Justin called back. "I might carry that heavy bag for you – for a price."

"No way," said Lisa. "I know your 'prices.' I can't afford any more pizzas for you!"

"Here we are! Lucky me, no ticket!" Eliana

said as she opened her van parked at the curb. They all piled in with their bags.

"It's great to be in Rio again!" Marco said. "I can feel the *carioca* (carry-OH-ca) spirit already."

"What does carioca mean?" Juan asked.

"A carioca is a person who is happy, carefree, loves life, loves people. And he or she has to be born in Rio. Like my sister. Eliana is a true carioca," Marco laughed.

"Can we go to Ipanema this afternoon?" Lisa asked Marco. "I can't wait to see it."

"Sure," said Marco. "And I can't wait to show it to you."

"Oh, what traffic today!" Eliana said. "Saturdays are always bad. Almost 6 million people in Rio and all heading for the beach. You will be lucky to find a tiny patch of sand! But Carlos and Éva will take good care of you!"

"We are coming into the part of Rio called Centro now," Marco said. "The first Portugese colony began here. You can still see some of the old houses tucked into quiet little streets among the skyscrapers."

"Look! Over there is our *Teatro Municipal* (tay-AH-tro mu-neece-i-PAL) (Municipal Theatre)," said Eliana. She pointed to a beautiful old stone building before them. "It is modeled after the Paris *Opéra* (o-PAY-ra). Rio has some wonderful buildings, doesn't it?"

"Yes, it really does. Is it still the capitol of

Brazil?" Lisa asked.

"No, Brazilia is now the capitol. It is about 600 miles northwest of here. But Rio looks like a capitol city, doesn't it? And it is still the heart of Brazilian culture," said Eliana.

"Look how close we are to Sugar Loaf now!" said Justin. "I can see the little cable car going along the wire."

"*Little* is right! Lisa and I may stay on the beach!" Amy said.

"Oh, you *must* go up Pâo de Açúcar! It is the most wonderful treat in Rio. Even I go up. And I am afraid of high places!" laughed Eliana. "Ask my children!"

"I know another wonderful treat in Rio.

"Look how close we are to Sugar Loaf. I can see the little cable car going along the wire."

And it is going to be my surprise for all of you," Marco announced.

"What? What? Tell us!" begged the kids.

"And ruin the surprise? Oh no. You'll see very soon. But I'm not telling!" Marco smiled a mysterious smile.

CHAPTER 3

Favelas and Beaches

"We're home!" Eliana opened the door to her apartment. "And here are my Éva and Carlos to greet you!" The girl and boy shook hands with everyone and hugged their uncle. Éva was small and blond, while Carlos was tall and dark like his mother.

"Wow, are you tan!" Lisa said to Éva. "I would love to get like that while I'm here!"

"Just spend a day on Ipanema with us," Carlos laughed. "The sun in Rio is magic!"

"And *very* hot," Marco said. "You kids must all put sunscreen on. Lots of it!"

They all stepped into the large sunny room filled with windows.

"Look at this view!" Miss Lake gasped. On one side was the bright blue ocean with a long white beach. Behind them were the mountains with dark green jungle below.

"See how close we are to Ipanema!" Éva said. "And it is really crowded today. We had better get down there!"

The beach was packed with brown bodies and bright-colored beach umbrellas.

"They're playing *soccer* on the beach!" Juan said. "Fantastic!"

"Come look out all over Rio," said Marco. "You can see the whole city from up here."

"What is the big white statue on top of that mountain?" Juan asked.

"Isn't it beautiful – the *Cristo* (CREE-sto)?" said Marco. "It was built in 1931 with money from churches all over Brazil."

They looked out at the tall statue of Christ standing with arms spread in welcome. All of Rio lay stretched out below.

"Can you go up there to the base of the statue?" Justin asked.

"Yes, it's a super trip up *Corcovado* (cor-co-VAD-o) Mountain," Carlos said. "It's 2400 feet high! You take a little train up. We'll do it while you're here!"

"The train sounds a lot better than the cable car on the wire!" Lisa said.

"I see so many shacks all over those hills," Amy said. "Right behind the highrises. There are thousands of them!"

"Those are the *favelas* (fa-VEL-as)," Éva explained. "Little town of shacks. Rio is full of them. They always make me feel sad. So many people here are very, very rich. But so many have nothing. You will see lots of children begging. Homeless children."

"It is a sad thing in Rio," Eliana said. "That this beautiful city has its dark side – people who are living with nothing."

"One thing is good, though: the beaches in Rio belong to *everyone,* rich or poor," said Marco.

Soon the kids were all heading out the door in swimsuits and t-shirts.

"Don't take *anything* valuable to the beach," Marco said. "Just a few *cruzieros* (crew-ZAY-ros) for drinks and ice cream."

"Marco, when are you going to tell us about our surprise?" Juan asked. "Is it tonight? You've got to tell us!"

"Oh, no! You'll find out soon enough!" Marco said. "Go hit the beach now!"

"We will have a big Brazilian dinner ready for you," said Eliana. "Save room!"

"*Até logo!* (ah-tay-LOW-go) (see you later)!" Carlos said as he shut the door.

They all got into the elevator.

"Marco won't tell us *anything*!" said Justin. "I wonder what the surprise is. Maybe we're going to a famous restaurant?"

"You would pick that!" Lisa laughed.

"Well, you'd probably pick a tour of a bikini factory!" said Justin.

"Maybe he's introducing us to Pelé!" said Juan. "Now that would be the best!"

"My uncle loves surprises," Éva said. "And you can never get him to tell."

"Ground floor!" Carlos announced. "Ipanema, here we come!"

CHAPTER 4

Wipe Out!

"This is amazing!" said Lisa as the kids stepped out on the sand of Ipanema beach. "Totally people! How do you ever find a place to sit?"

"Oh, today isn't bad. You should see it in the summer!" Éva said. "Come on. We always find a spot over here."

The kids picked their way among bright-colored beach umbrellas and tanned, oiled sunbathers.

"I can't believe the bikinis here!" said

"This is amazing!" said Lisa as the kids stepped on the sands of Ipanema Beach.

Amy. "They are so tiny!"

"Oh, we all wear them in Rio," said Éva. "The beach uniform."

"I'm glad we bought new ones in Venezuela! But they're not *this* little!" laughed Lisa.

"Is that ice cream they're selling?" Justin asked. "I'm getting some." He headed for a red and white umbrella on the beach.

"It never takes Justin long to check out the food," Juan laughed. "Hey, is that volleyball they're playing over there? It's crazy! They don't use their hands! Just heads and feet! That might be fun!"

"There's a *pelada* (pel-AH-da), Juan."

23

Carlos pointed to a soccer match set up on the beach. "These guys are really good."

"I sure wish we could see a match at Maracana," Juan said.

"Impossible. The tickets are sold out," said Carlos. "Two big teams are playing now."

Éva set down her beach bag. "This is a good spot. We're close to the water when we want to cool off." Amy and Lisa threw down their towels beside hers.

"Tell Justin we went down to where the good waves are," Carlos told his sister. He and Juan walked on down the beach.

"Some of them are really good out there! And that surf is something else!" said Juan.

They watched guys catch some large waves.

Suddenly Justin yelled to them. He had an ice cream in one hand, a drink in the other.

"How are you going to surf with all that stuff in your hands?" laughed Carlos.

"I am amazing," said Justin. "Juan knows. Food gives me superhuman powers."

"O.K., Superhuman, come on out when you finish eating. We'll trade off on the boards," Carlos told him. Then he and Juan waded out into the waves with their bogey boards.

They lay on their boards waiting for a good wave to come along. Suddenly Carlos yelled, "This is it!" and the wave caught him! He was off on his board, racing towards the beach. Juan watched him go. He had missed the wave. But there would be another one.

Then he saw Justin coming towards him. He had Carlos' board and was paddling out into the surf. 'Oh, no,' thought Juan. 'There's a wave coming right at him! It's going to wipe him out!'

Suddenly a huge wave broke on top of Justin and he disappeared! His board went flying. Finally Juan saw the top of Justin's head lift up out of the water. He quickly paddled over to his friend.

"Wow, you really got buried, man! You O.K.?" Juan asked.

Justin spat out a mouthful of water. "Oh,

sure. But these South American waves are something else! Now let's find that board!"

"Here comes Carlos. He's got it!" said Juan.

"Hey, Justin, you want to get those waves *behind* you!" Carlos yelled. "Come on. I'll show you how to get a good ride."

"Wait! There's Lisa coming in. I bet she wants to share my board," Juan said. "I didn't plan on this!"

"And there's Amy right behind her," Carlos groaned. "I thought they were just going to sunbathe!"

CHAPTER 5

Marco's Surprise!

"Lots of red faces tonight!" said Eliana as they all sat down at dinner together. "You see what I mean about the Rio sun? I hope it does not hurt too much?"

"Oh, no," said Justin. "Wow, this dinner looks fantastic! And I'm really hungry!"

"Pain disappears when Justin sees food," Lisa laughed.

"And who shared his bogey board with you today?" asked Justin.

"Amy and Lisa were pretty good out there," Carlos said. "Not too many girls bogey board at Ipanema. Lots of guys were watching."

"These American girls are pretty amazing," Marco laughed. "Full of surprises!"

"Speaking of *surprises*!" said Juan. "Marco, we've waited long enough!"

"After dinner. Then you'll find out," Marco laughed. "Look at this beautiful dinner my sister has made for us! Tell us what everything is, Eliana!"

"For our guests I have made a special Brazilian dish called *feijoada* (feh-JWA-da)." Eliana pointed to a large bowl before her. "It is a stew made of black beans, beef and pork. You put it over the rice. Delicious!"

"And try these!" Carlos pointed to long metal sticks with pieces of meat on them.

"When I write home about this dinner it's going to take *two* postcards!" Justin said.

Finally everybody sat back in their chairs. The bowls of food were nearly empty.

"*Maraviloso* (mar-a-vee-LOH-so), Eliana!" said Marco. "What a wonderful dinner!"

"Oh, you must all have *sorvette* (sor-VETTE) now," Eliana said. "Ice cream!"

"But Marco has to tell us the surprise first," Juan said. "He promised."

"Is dinner over?" asked Marco.

"Please!!!" said Juan.

"Well," Marco began. "A friend of mine had some tickets to give away. I said I had some special American guests in town. I said they *might* be interested in these tickets."

"Tell us!" said Amy.

"These tickets are very hard to get," Marco said. "Especially this weekend."

"Maracana! You got tickets for a game!" cried Juan. "Is that it? Maracana?"

"Well, is that where the soccer match is in Rio tonight?" Marco smiled happily.

Everybody cheered and got up from the table.

"Dessert later!" they all agreed. Even Justin!

CHAPTER 6

Maracana!

"The lights of Rio are coming on all around you," Eliana said. "Look at the Christo. It is all lit up. It is a pretty drive to Maracana."

"I never thought I'd get to see a game down here!" said Juan. "This is so neat."

"The best Rio soccer club is playing a great team from Santos tonight," Marco said.

"Will Tito play tonight?" Juan asked.

"Yes, he plays for the best club in Rio," Carlos said. "Tito is so *fast*!"

"He's the player I've heard about so much," Juan said. "This will be so great!"

"Carlos and Éva, do you remember this street from *Carnaval* (Kahr-nah-VAHL)?" asked Eliana. "This is where you joined the parade."

"Yes! Oh, that was so neat," said Éva. "Guys, you have to come down for Carnaval next year. It is just the best!"

"What is Carnaval?" asked Lisa.

"It's the biggest party in the world," Marco said. "Rio just explodes. It happens just before Lent, in our hot mid-summer here. No one sleeps for four days."

"People really dress up to dance the samba (SUHM-buh) in the parades," Eliana said.

"Some save all year to buy one costume. Éva is right – you must come for Carnaval."

"I'm coming! Count me in!" said Miss Lake. "I love the samba!"

"We're coming, too!" cried Lisa.

"But what about school?" said Miss Lake.

"You have school, too!" Justin said.

"Oh, me? Well, teachers are allowed special vacations at certain times." Miss Lake smiled. "Carnaval is one of those times!"

"Everybody comes together at Carnaval," Eliana said. "All the different kinds of people here: Indians, Blacks, Portugese, like us. All these groups intermarried and formed *more* groups, so Rio has it all!"

"Wait till you see Maracana," Carlos told the kids and their teacher. "It's the greatest stadium in the world! It holds 2 hundred thousand people!"

"This is where Pelé was king in the 1950's and 60's," Eliana said.

"Marco, did you ever get to see Pelé play?" Juan asked.

"Oh, yes! Many times! He was a thrill to watch," said Marco. "He could make his body do amazing things with a soccer ball!"

"Our soccer coach always talks about Pelé. She showed us some of his special tricks for kicking goals," Lisa said.

Suddenly horns began honking all around

the van. People were shouting and waving their fists as more and more cars appeared.

"What if we're late? Will they still let us in?" Juan stared at his watch.

"Don't worry, we'll make it," Marco said.

"There's the garage now," said Eliana. "When we get out of the van, stay close to each other. The crowds *really* push!"

"It's easy to get lost. Our section is 50 E if we get separated," Marco told everybody.

Finally they were parked and joined the noisy crowds pouring into the stadium.

"I feel like I'm being just swept along. I hardly need to move my feet!" said Amy.

"Hang on, Amy. Don't fall down in this

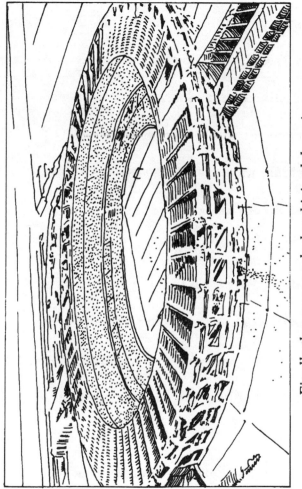

Finally they were parked and joined the noisy crowds pouring into the stadium.

crowd," Marco warned. He grabbed her arm.

Suddenly they were inside the stadium. They looked down onto a faraway bright green field in the center of a huge circle of seats.

Juan stared. "This place is *huge*!"

Marco led everyone down closer and closer to the field. Finally they reached their row.

"These are great seats, Marco!" Carlos shouted. "Wow! We're really near the field."

"Here come the players!" Juan yelled.

The crowd roared and waved their flags. Players in bright-colored shirts and shorts ran onto the field.

"The Rio club is in the yellow and green shirts and blue shorts," Marco explained.

"I see Tito! The tallest one with the long blond hair. I can't believe it's him! Marco, this is the best!" said Juan.

"They're starting!" cried Carlos. "There goes Tito with the ball. Look how fast he is!"

People screamed, "*Goll! Goll* (goal)!"

The line of green and yellow shirts raced down the field towards the goal posts.

"Watch Tito go right by everybody. No one can stop him!" said Juan.

"Oh, no! They got the ball away from him!" cried Lisa. "Take it back, Tito!"

"He's got it again! He's going to shoot!" yelled Marco.

Suddenly there was a terrible loud *bam*! It

was just above their heads. Smoke and showers of sparks.

"Watch out! Firecrackers!" Carlos yelled. "Tito made a goal!"

The crowd screamed, "Tito! Tito!"

More firecrackers exploded overhead!

"Cover your faces!" cried Marco.

"They're starting again! There's the kick," yelled Juan.

The score was tied up by halftime. The crowd was roaring with excitement.

"Stay in your seats," Marco said. "It's a madhouse during halftime."

"I'll call the ice cream guy," Justin waved to the man with the sorvette sign.

Suddenly Juan saw a man selling postcards and flags. He was just in the next aisle. It would be easy to get over there. Then he could tell the guys he bought the postcards *at* Marcana! Yes! He jumped up from his end seat and ran up the steps.

But suddenly Juan stopped. He couldn't move. The aisle was filled with people pressing in on him! He could barely breathe! Someone started pushing! Juan felt himself begin to fall forward. What if he went down? He would be trampled! He had to stay standing! Now he was leaning, leaning. Where was the floor? He could no longer feel it under his feet! He was hot, hotter, dizzy.

Suddenly Juan felt somebody grab his arm – hard! They were pulling him back up. They were pushing everybody away from him. It was Marco! He was picking Juan up now, out of the crowd, carrying him away. Where there was air.

"Juan! You scared me! I saw you going down in the crowd. I couldn't get to you!" Marco cried. He hugged Juan tightly.

"I'm sorry. Really sorry," Juan gasped. "I saw a guy selling postcards. He was so close. I thought I could just run over and get them. And then all the people came. It was awful."

"That's the dangerous thing about these big soccer crowds. Suddenly you can get swept up into one and you're powerless," Marco said. "I know. It happened to me."

"It did?" asked Juan.

"Yes, and I think it was the time when I went after souvenirs by myself." Marco smiled. "Come on! Let's go back to the others. After the game I'll take you to get postcards for your friends. Do you think they might like them autographed?"

"Autographed? How?" asked Juan.

"Didn't Carlos and Éva tell you my surprises come in pairs?" laughed Marco. "I have arranged a special meeting for after the match. I think you will like the person who is coming!"

"Who? Who?" cried Juan. "Not – not –

Tito?"

"Well, I guess I could try to get somebody else if . . ."

Juan let out a yell. "All right! Tito! I'm going to meet Tito! Marco, you are the best!"

"Come on back to our seats. And promise me one thing, Juan." Marco smiled.

"What's that?"

"You will stay *glued* to your seat till the end of this match!" They both laughed and then headed back to their friends.